This way please!

# Dear Santa

By Amy Husband

First published in 2010
by Meadowside Children's Books
185 Fleet Street London EC4A 2HS
www.meadowsidebooks.com

Text © Rachel Elliot
Illustrations © Amy Husband
The rights of Amy Husband and Rachel
Elliot to be identified as the author and
illustrator of this work have been
asserted by them in accordance with the
Copyright, Designs and Patents Act, 1988

A CIP catalogue record for this book
is available from the British Library
10 9 8 7 6 5 4 3 2 1
Printed in China

meadowside
CHILDREN'S BOOKS

Holly Hall
Christmas Lane
The North Pole

1st December

Dear boys and girls,

It's my favourite time of year again. I'm writing to find out
what you would like for Christmas.

The most important thing to remember is that you must be very,
very good. I hear about everything you do on the parent hotline,
and naughty boys and girls won't be getting any presents at all.
Please fill in the attached slip or write to me!!

## Love Santa

P.S. Mrs Santa, the elves and Rudolph all say Hi!

Dear Santa,
This year I have been:

☐ good
☐ bad
☐ other (please explain)...

For Christmas I would like:

☐ a surprise
☐ nothing at all
☐ other (please explain)...

# Dear Santa,

Thank you for your letter. I ran out of space on the slip, so I'm writing instead. I have been <u>mostly good</u> this year, but Mum and I went to the shops today and bought an Advent calendar to remind me to be especially good <u>from now on</u>. I didn't know about the parent hotline. I hope we can start from today. I promise to be <u>**really**</u> good. What I'd like for Christmas is a new ~~red~~ red bike with a <u>Very</u> Loud Bell, please!

From **Michael**

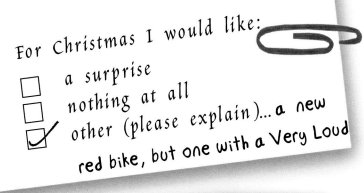

P.S. Mum says that this is going to be the Best Christmas Ever! She said  something about a new addition, I think she must mean my new red bike!

Dear Santa,
This year I have been:

☑ good

☐ bad

☒ other (please explain)...
~~I was a bit naughty last Tue~~

For Christmas I would like:

☐ a surprise

☐ nothing at all

☑ other (please explain)... a new red bike, but one with a Very Loud

Look, my Advent calendar has an Angel in it and Mum says I have to be like one for ALL of Advent.    ⟶

# Dear Santa,

I'm writing to say sorry because there was a bit of a mishap today. Mum was chatting and I was <u>REALLY</u> bored, but I didn't mean for Bruno's lead to get tangled around (all) those legs. It was just funny ~~that~~ seeing him pretend to be a bird.

If I'm not allowed to have the red bike after all that falling over, could I have new clothes please? People keep sending us old ones, but they're too small for me and they're **all** pink!

From **Michael**

Today, I had a robin, like the ones in the park! ⟶

# Dear Santa,

I'm writing to explain about the noisy game. Mum was asleep and Dad was reading the papers. I went to play the noisy game in the garden with Bruno. We forgot about Mum being asleep! I was winning when Mum opened her bedroom window, wearing her **crossest expression**. I expect I can't have new clothes now, but could I have a drum instead? (Just a small one?) Dad says it's okay, as long as Mum is **always** out when I play it.

# From Michael

P.S. Mum had pickled onions, peanut butter and chillies for lunch today! Yuck!

I wish it would snow, then we could make a snowman, which wouldn't be noisy at all!

# Dear Santa,

Mum and Dad decorated the nursery today. I think they're going to turn it into a playroom for me and my little brother! I did <u>try</u> to be good and help. I'm really sorry about all the glue on the carpet but Bruno got a bit <u>over-excited</u>. I expect ▓▓ I'm not allowed the drum now, so please may I have a train set for the new playroom instead?

From
# Michael

my little brother, Tommy

P.S. I wish Christmas would hurry up! Mum says she can't give me a piggyback until after Christmas.

There was a bauble in my calendar this morning, but Dad says we have to wait a while before we decorate our tree after the 'decorating disaster' today.

**Dear Santa,**

It was great fun to see you at your grotto! I know you said I could probably have the train set but... well, there was another mishap. Granny and Grandad have arrived and everyone is asleep <u>all the time</u>. Granny keeps telling Mum to rest, but Mum gets more naps than Grandad at the moment! Anyway, Bruno and I just wanted them to play disguises with us. I promise I won't draw on anyone again. If I'm definitely not allowed the train set, could I just have a book?

From **Michael**

P.S. If I am allowed a book, could I have one about disguises?

Look, a reindeer like the ones we saw today outside the grotto! →

# Dear Santa,

We all decorated the tree today! It looked ⸱brilliant⸱ but then something bad happened. Bruno ate <u>all the chocolates.</u> I tried to hide the wrappers, but Mum found them, so I'm on the naughty step. (Bruno is in the garden too, partly because he's in disgrace and partly ▓ because he's been sick.) I know I won't be allowed a book any more, so can I just have some more chocolates for the tree?

## From Michael

P.S. Dad's brought my old cot down from the loft. I think he's going to make Bruno sleep in it so he can't eat the tree chocolates again.

The tree in today's Advent picture isn't as good as ours!

20

# Dear Santa,

I just saw Grandad pick up the phone, so I thought I had better write and explain in case he was calling the parent hotline. Granny and Grandad took me carol singing today.  Granny did tell me to stay still, but I just wanted to <u>investigate the dark a bit</u>. I only picked one candle up, but they were all sort of attached. Mum says not to ask for chocolates because Bruno will just eat them again, so could I just have a torch please?

From **Michael**

P.S. Mum and Dad keep reading names out loud. It's so boring! Could you send them a story book for Christmas?

Today's Advent picture was you!  →

# Dear Santa,

Today Mum let me help her decorate our cake. It was Bruno's idea to check the marzipan was <u>tasty</u>. I didn't think Mum would notice, but she did. If I'm not allowed a torch now, can you please just make Mum's tummy smaller so she's easier to cuddle!?

### From **Michael**

P.S. It's nearly Christmas Eve and I want to try to stay awake to say hello, but Mum says you won't come if I don't go to sleep. Is that true?

Look, my Advent picture was of a Christmas cake too, I'm keeping it away from Bruno though!

# Dear Santa,

Dad just said something about the <u>parent hotline,</u> and he wasn't smiling, so I'm writing to explain. Dad said he wanted to go for a ride on Christmas Day, so I cleaned his bike as a present. I didn't know the little screws that rolled away were important. I know I haven't been very good, so could I please just have a Very Loud Bell for Christmas? (I'll try to be good enough for the red bike next year.)

### From **Michael**

P.S. We're going to hospital now! Dad says there's a big Christmas surprise there, so we've left your mince pies and carrots in the fridge.

I really hope I'm allowed a present. I'm on my best behaviour today, I <u>double promise.</u>

Holly Hall
Christmas Lane
The North Pole

25th December

Dear Michael,

# Merry Christmas!

Thank you for all your letters. Our post-elf has been kept very busy! As you were aware, things were not looking good for your Christmas list. However, a last-minute call on the parent hotline has changed everything. I heard how helpful you were when your Mum was in hospital having your new baby sister. You've completely made up for all the 'mishaps'. You'll find your present underneath the Christmas tree.

## Love Santa

P.S. I hope that the bell is loud enough. My elves had to wear earmuffs to test it!

P.P.S. Your Mum is right. I wouldn't have come if you hadn't gone to sleep, so it's just as well you were so tired!